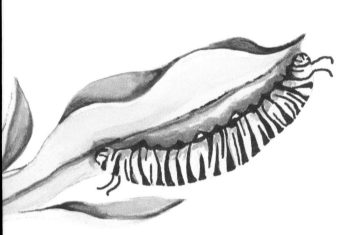

This book belongs to:

_____

There's A Day Out There

Written and Illustrated by
Sharon Goldman

For Lily and Mary Kate,

Go outside and see what
nature has for you!

Sharon Goldman
April 25, 2019

Tooly Woo
PUBLISHING

Ponte Vedra Beach, Florida

Book and cover design by Sagaponack Books & Design

ISBNs:
978-0-9600897-0-3 (softcover)
978-0-9600897-1-0 (hardcover)
978-0-9600897-2-7 (e-book)

Library of Congress Control Number: 2019901668

Summary: Nature invites a young boy to come outdoors to learn about the world waiting outside his window.

JUV029010 Juvenile Fiction / Science & Nature / Environment
JUV039090 Juvenile Fiction / Social Themes / New Experience
JUV029020 Juvenile Fiction / Science & Nature / Weather
JUV002300 Juvenile Fiction / Animals / Butterflies, Moths & Caterpillars
JUV051000 Juvenile Fiction / Imagination & Play

Printed and bound in the United States of America
First Edition

Acknowledgments

Thanks to the Goldman family who opened my eyes to the world outside and helped me recognize the different species of local flora and fauna in their natural habitats.

I'd also like to thank Frances Keiser, Stacey G. Sather, and Marilyn Baron for their encouragement, patience, and expertise in helping me create this book.

For my husband, Richard, who taught our daughters about the great outdoors, how to identify birds, the proper way to pitch a tent (and fold it back), and his attempts at getting them interested in fishing.

*The best thing one can do when it's raining
is to let it rain.*

—Henry Wadsworth Longfellow

"Mom, there's nothing to do."

"Would you like to go outside?" answered Mom.

"There's a wondrous day out there waiting for us."

As I looked out my window,
I heard a tiny voice.

"Come outside,"
laughed the ladybug.

"There's a day out here!

"Come away from that window
and visit it from my side.

"Haven't you heard, it's good luck
when you see one of me?"

"Come outside,"
said a shimmering voice.

"There's a day out here!

"I can add some yellows, if you're blue.

"I'll follow you with my sun rays wherever you go and try not to cast too big a shadow."

"Come outside,"
said a muffled voice
from inside a chrysalis.

"There's a day out here!

"It's time for me to turn into a beautiful Indian leaf butterfly.

"You must come out now before I'm camouflaged and look like any leaf on a twig. You might walk by and never notice me."

"Come outside,"
whispered the wind softly.

"There's a day out here!

"I'll swirl around you,
gently lift you off your feet and
tickle your toes while I'm at it."

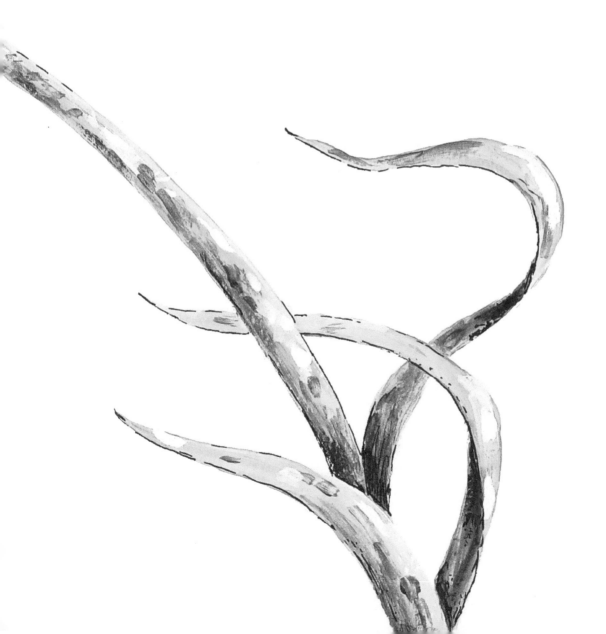

"Come outside,"
chirped a baby wren.

"There's a day out here!

"I need someone to see my first flight.

"My mother is off finding worms
and I can't wait another minute
to spread my wings."

"Come outside,"
chanted the ocean.

"There's a day out here!

"Take a walk to the beach.
I'm over here! I'm over here!

"I'll keep waving until you
wave back."

"Come outside,"
tap-tap-tapped something
on the window.

"There's a day out here!

"Look up at the only little rain cloud in the sky.

"It's me!

"I'll cool you off with the mist of a light sunshower."

"But I don't think my mother will want to go out in the rain," I said.

"Ask her," cried the cloud.

"Ask her," chanted the wave.

"Ask her," chirped the wren.

"Ask her," whispered the wind.

"Ask her," fluttered the butterfly.

"Ask her," shimmered the sun.

"Good luck," laughed the ladybug.

"Mom, can we go outside now?"
I asked.

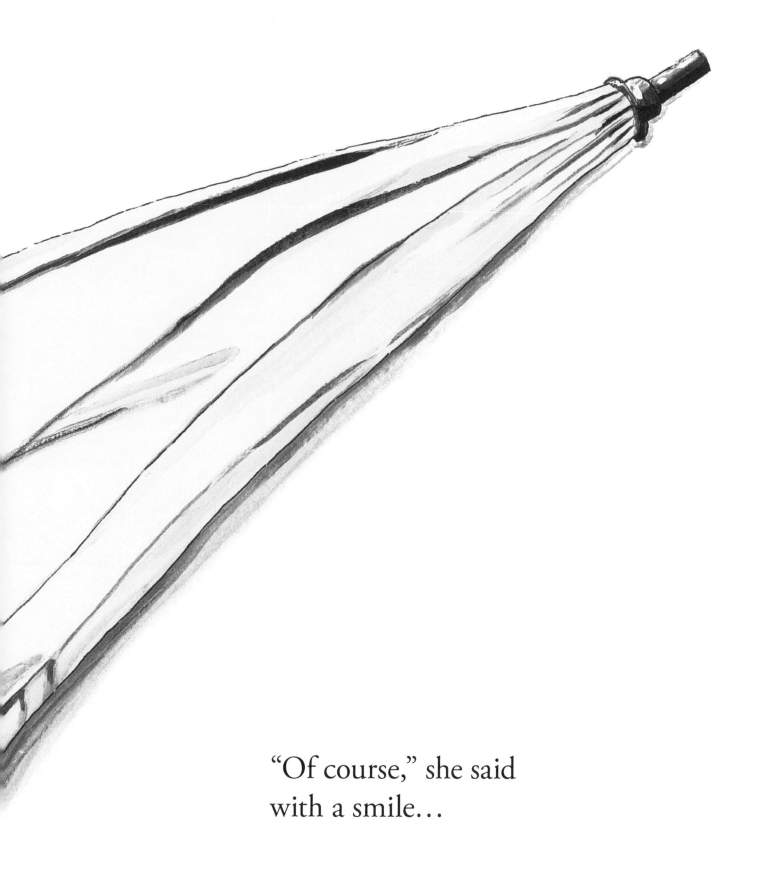

"Of course," she said
with a smile…

as wide as an

open umbrella.

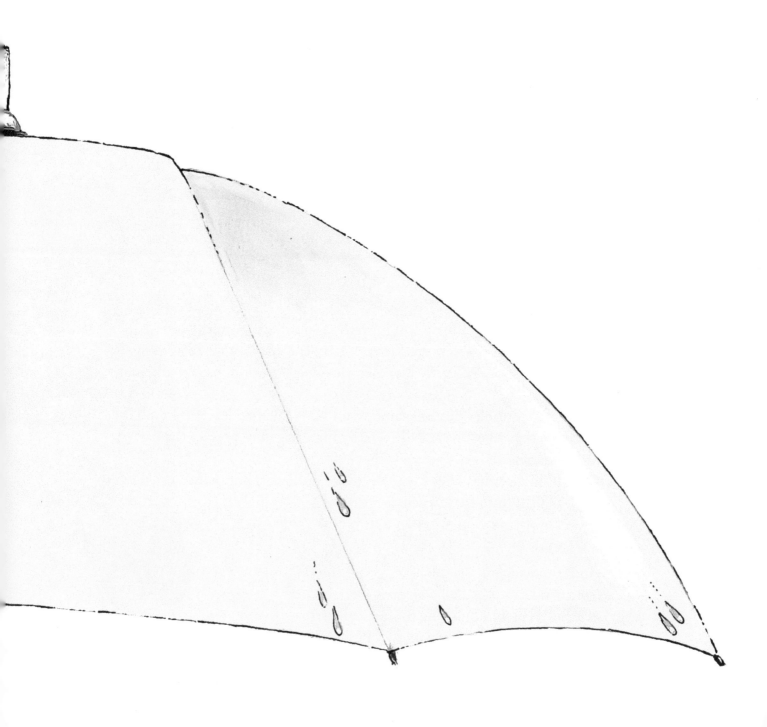

Fun Facts!

LADYBUGS:
- Ladybugs are in the family of small beetles.
- Ladybugs are helpful. They eat aphids and other insects that damage plants.
- A single ladybug can eat up to 50 aphids a day!
- Male ladybugs are also called ladybugs, not "gentlemanbugs!"
- Ladybugs can be different colors: brown, black, orange, gray, yellow, red, and pink.
- In some countries, ladybugs are a sign of good luck.
- Ladybugs clean themselves after every meal. I hope they don't forget to wash behind their antennas!
- Some ladybugs do not have spots, while others may have up to 20 spots.
- Female ladybugs can lay up to 1,000 eggs in their lifetime.

THE SUN AND SHADOWS:
- The sun is a star and is the closest star to the earth.
- It takes eight minutes for light from the sun to reach the earth.
- Your shadow is the longest in the late afternoon and early morning.
- Go outside with an adult and try looking at shadows at different times of the day. It's fun!

INDIAN LEAF BUTTERFLIES:
- Another name for an Indian leaf butterfly is dead-leaf butterfly.
- Even though Indian leaf butterflies can have colorful tips on their wings, when they close them tightly together, the wings are dull, brown and look like dead leaves.
- Indian leaf butterflies can hide among millions of fallen leaves, or land on a branch and look like one leaf. They are camouflaged to protect themselves from predators.
- Indian leaf butterflies like to eat the nectar of flowers but prefer rotten fruit that has fallen from trees. Yucky!

THE WIND:

- Wind is moving air.
- A soft wind can be called a breeze.
- Little bursts of wind moving fast are called gusts.
- A hurricane has very strong wind. Hang on!

- Windmills turn wind into useful work like making electricity or pumping water from under the ground.
- Large groups of wind turbines are called wind farms. No cows there!
- Wind helps sailboats move without a motor.
- Wind is a clean and renewable energy. That is a good thing!

WRENS:

- Another name for a wren is "cave dweller." They got that name because their nests look like a caves.
- Both male and female wrens are brown. Their bills are short and curve downward.
- Wrens have a VERY loud song. If you are close to one, cover your ears!
- Wrens eat spiders and insects while hopping and dashing along the ground.
- Wrens lay between one and nine eggs. Only the female incubates the eggs, but both adults will feed the young chicks.

OCEANS:

- The five oceans of the world are the Pacific, Atlantic, Indian, Southern, and Arctic.
- The Pacific Ocean is the largest ocean. It covers a third of the earth's surface.
- The Atlantic Ocean is the second largest ocean in the world. It's about half the size of the Pacific Ocean.
- The Indian Ocean is located between Africa and Southern Asia. It has the largest breeding ground of humpback whales.
- The Southern Ocean is located around the South Pole. It's home to the Emperor Penguin and Wandering Albatross.
- The Arctic Ocean is the smallest ocean. It's located at the northernmost part of our planet and it's very cold. *Brrrrr!*
- Polar bears swim in the icy waters of the Arctic Ocean.

CLOUDS:

- Clouds are made up of millions of tiny water droplets.
- Snow, sleet, hail, and rain fall from clouds. It's called precipitation. Get your umbrella!
- The three types of clouds are cumulus, which are puffy, cirrus which are thin and wispy, and stratus which are layered and flat.

Look out your window. What do you see?

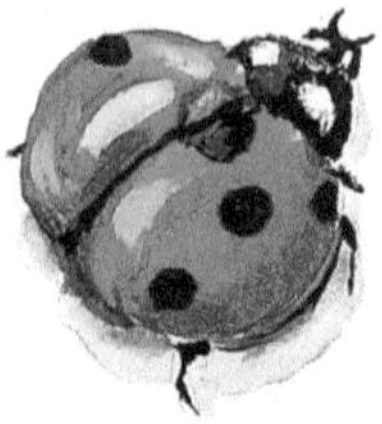

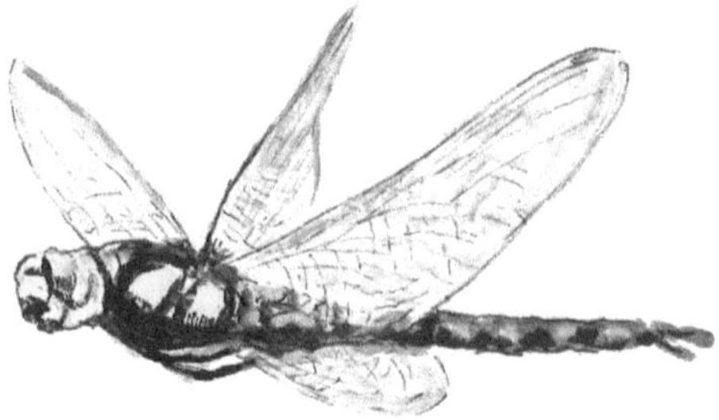

_____

_____

_____

_____

_____

_____

_____

_____

_____

_____

_____

Go Outside!

Explore what nature has for you
And take a closer look,
In your backyard or neighborhood
And don't forget this book.

Invite a grown-up for some fun
To venture out with you.
Look for bugs and birds and trees
And those are just a few.

Did you find a ladybug
A beetle or a bee?
See a dragonfly fly by
A hawk or chickadee?

What color were the flowers,
If any, that you found?
Were they blooming on the trees
Or planted in the ground?

Did you spy a spider
Weaving a fine web?
Did an insect get away
Or was it caught instead?

Did you luck upon a lizard,
A snail or jumping frog?
I bet you saw a kitty cat
And pet a friendly dog.

Did you come upon a squirrel
Or pretty butterfly?
Were you caught in the rain,
Or was it nice and dry?

I guess it's time to go back home,
I'm sure you'd like to stay.
But you can always go outside
On another day.

Coloring Page

Coloring Page

About the Author/Artist

As a native Floridian, Sharon Goldman has been surrounded by water, whether it is the ocean, a spring or a swimming pool. She strives to create work that captures the spirit of Florida and her love of nature. Many of her paintings are of birds, vegetation, landscapes, and seascapes as well as underwater swimmers. Her colorful palette and background as a designer and art director help her envision her novel compositions. She describes her work as painterly realism.

A graduate of the University of Florida in Fine Arts, Sharon had a long career in the advertising business. After having three children (now college graduates), she started a new career teaching art after school in her home studio and has taught more than 200 children in her community. She also shows her paintings in galleries throughout Northeast Florida and has had several solo shows.

As an empty nester, Sharon has more time to work on her creative endeavors such as writing and illustrating children's books. She has also coauthored a romance novel and a musical with her sister. The creative process is what gets her going in the morning and sometimes keeps her up at night while thinking about her next idea.

Sharon and her husband Richard, a nature enthusiast, live in Ponte Vedra Beach, Florida. When time permits, he likes to fish in the backyard lagoon, while Sharon, phone in hand, is ready to capture the photo of his next giant bass. Of course, he throws it back.

For more about Sharon and to view her art, visit:

www.SharonGoldmanArt.com

CPSIA information can be obtained
at www.ICGtesting.com
Printed in the USA
LVHW012344280319
612266LV00005B/46/P

9 780960 089703